REFERENCE GUIDE

OI. REFERENCE GUIDE
OII. COPYWRITE
OIII. PRE-AMBLE
1. PRETTY DOGGY
2. IN THE DARK
3. TONIGHT WE BECOME MEN
4. IT SNOWS IN MIAMI
5. JACK-KNIFE
6. WHEN THE BOUGH BREAKS
7. FAULTY REFLECTIONS
8. A BEAUTIFUL DAY
9. LOST AND FOUND
10. WELCOME HOME
11. CLOUDS OF DESIRE
12. FOOD CHAIN
13. 14. THE TRAVELER YOU CAN'T KNOW
15. YOU KNEW
16. IMAGINE THAT
17. EXESTENTIAL ADMONITIONS
18. SHADOWS LIVE
19. KEEPING AMERICA FREE
20. 21. NO NOEL
22. 23. LET LOOSE THE RATS OF WAR
24. ALL SEGMENTS
25. RIDDLED
26. TWISTED DESTINY
27. NEIGHBORS
28. ...
29. I'LL SEE YOU THERE
30. THE SOUND OF PILLS
31. MONKEY ON MY BACK
32. IT'S ONLY FAIR
33. 34. PHILOSOPHY, DEEP OR NOT
35. ...
36. NEVER THE LESS
37. 38. WHISTLERS WALK
39. GET OFF MY BACK
40. WHAT IF 6 WERE 9
41. YOU'RE IN TOO DEEP
42. ...
43. MY TRAIN
44. TELLING TELLING TOLD
45. 46. A LADY ALONE
47. FRAGILE AS AN EGG

48. 49. 50. ARE WE THERE YET
51. FLY BEATNIK
52. THE EVE OF ALL HALLOWS
53. 54. UNDYING LOVE
55. THE REAL REAL
56. ...
57. HAPPY BIRTHDAY FAYE
58. OVERCOME
59. AT THE TABLE
60. GOD RIDES A HARLEY
61. A DAY IN THE PAST
62. GROW UP AND ROCK
63. IS
64. 65. 66. LAST JOURNAL
67. HOME SICK, SCHOOL SICK
68. ...
69. NEEDLE IN THE CAGE
70. I WOULD CRY FOR YOU
71. SHEMO
72. DREAM ON, DREAM ON
73. 74. IT REALLY HAPPENED
75. 76. 77. 78. 79. WHY I FIGHT
80. CANDY HAZE
81. THE WRATH OF GRAPES
82. 83. PEARL DUST
84. NO-ONE HERE
85. MAYBE, MAYBE NOT
86. 87. HE JUST DOESN'T UNDERSTAND ME
88. NANTUCKET BUCKET
89. I CRACK ME UP
90. SINK
91. I'M A RACEST
92. PLEASE DON'T LEAVE ME
93. A ZILLION RAINBOWS
94. QUICKSAND
95. CREDITS

A BOOK OF SKRYBES 1.3

A BOOK OF SKRYBES 1.3

For the most part, this book is not from the heart, but imagination.
 Some things are clearly reality. Others are real or real opinions, but are
exaggerated and or more intense so as not to be as personal and to really make
the point. Some skrybes have strong meaning, others…? Well you decide.
**If you think you're getting to know the writer of the skrybe, you're wasting
your time. That would only put a skew on the whole read and would make it
worthless!**
If you think you're getting in the writer's mind, be careful, you might hurt
yourself.
The reason for writing some skrybes was simply to test a writer's imagination or
ability to write as others do, as far as style and subject, like… poetry or greeting
card style, love and suicide.
I would think most readers would get the reason for the title:
DON'T CALL IT POETRY,
though like I said some skrybes do fit that criteria.

A goal of this book is to make even poetry interesting and enjoyable to read,
again. Hopefully the reader will enjoy the read even if the meaning or subject is
not clear (a large part of this book's endeavor), as well as writing in a manner
that could be interpreted as the reader's mind dictates.
IS YOUR IMAGINATION SUFFICIENT?
It's possible that you won't like some skrybe subject or content but I'm certain
you WILL read it again.
I believe that everyone can get a lot from this book.

Are you willing to go for a ride?

PRETTY DOGGY

That isn't a dog you're about to pet; it isn't rabies you might get.
Chances are you will get bit. Chances are you'll live forever and you won't like it.
You probably won't remember the people you kill, but someone will.
Running and hiding, a life of lies; and no matter what you do, the full moon will rise.

You lock yourself up; no one understands. 'Why do these chains bind your hands'?
When the sun comes up you'll be ok. "Please God, no more"; you'll daily pray.

Relief is possible, but where will you find a bullet made of silver? And who will use it?
No one will believe you; your words are bait. They'll see for themselves when the
full moon rises, then it's too late.

Month after month, year after year; the hunger grows and so does the fear.
Time won't stand still, it'll happen again; you'll participate in the deadly sin.

Don't pet the dog; don't look him in the eyes. His tail might not wag, but no one dies.

IN THE DARK

The darkness waits in silence: showing nothing, hearing all.
Encompassing the totality of your existence.
Outside and in; so thick you can barely move, and it keeps on going.
Run hard run fast. Watch your step; oblivion is shaky and obscure at best.
The end is close but no closer than when you started.
It's all behind you now: left, right, up, down and still ahead.
Keep on going, what could it hurt?
Dodge the shadows if you perceive them without light,
For there is no light in the void.
So comfortable and full of fear.
It makes no sense this unquantifiable emptiness.
If only you could be in control, but you're not.
How could you when the light continually eludes you?
How sad when it is so much closer than the dark.

TONIGHT WE BECOME MEN

I never knew that night could be so dark. I never knew there were so many stars.
The silence is so loud it almost hurts. All there is to hear is the wind blowing
through the trees and the occasional howl, screech or growl from some animal that
is obviously stalking us for dinner.
There's something in the bushes. If only we had a fire. In the movies they always
say fire will keep the scary beasts away. · How do you light a fire without gas and
a lighter?
What did your mom give us to eat? · How are we going to cook hot dogs without a
microwave or oven?
Something is coming out of the trees. Maybe we should run. Better yet let's just
hide. It might simply pass us by. I can see the hairy beast creeping up on us. Shine
your flashlight let's see. Are you supposed to stare into the eyes of the beast or do
raccoons take that as a challenge?
Set up the tent your mom gave you, that should protect us. Don't panic, I'm sure we
can figure it out, though a YouTube video on tents would help.
Why did you bring spikes in the tent bag · and how is a hammer going to help us set
up a tent?
This is too much. It might get down to sixty degrees tonight. Let's just clear a space
and the three of us can huddle together and use the tent as a blanket. Every movie
I've seen makes it clear, the best way to keep warm in a situation like this is to strip
down completely and huddle close to share body heat. I won't tell anyone if you guys
won't.
Hey guys wake up it's daytime. We made it. It's all over. We're real men!
Now we can go home and get something to eat. Tomorrow we'll tell the kids at
school how we braved the elements (whatever those are) fought off the wild beasts
and conquered the wilderness.
Look at these little footprints all over the place. Hey, what happened to our clothes?
Now what are we going to do? It'll be a long nude bike ride home; and most of it is
very public. We can't stay out here for the rest of our lives... Can we?
I don't think our man story is going to sound quite the same now.

IT SNOWS IN MIAMI

It starts with a possum under your porch, which is not so unusual; this is Florida.
A snake in your jeep and one in your front yard; a gator in your pool and a turtle
walking down the road. All kinds of birds everywhere and lizards like you've never seen.
The food in your pantry no longer safe from the hordes of mice out of seemingly nowhere.
Look at the pretty bunny and the family of ducks crossing the quiet neighborhood street.
None of these alone would be strange but this is not the forest and this is not normal!

When the snow begins to fall, you realize what's going on; the snow is black and the heat
 persists. - Foot prints in black from the accumulating snow on the ground. -
Stay inside; don't breathe it in; because the black air is dense.
There's an orange glow in the distant smoke filled sky.
No more mystery and nothing you can do.

THE GLADES ARE ON FIRE

JACK-KNIFE

Jack-knife, jack-knife, shiny steel and power. Pivot slick and strong.
Click, click, fold, unfold. It's not your aspiration. Straight, strong and
able to hold, to reach your destination.
Shiny glare in darkest night. Slippery wet, your need to fight.
Start to fold, it's not the time. Hold it strong and true.
Grip in hand, still no control. The street's controlling you.
Violent crash, twist the steel, no longer shiny clean.
Flashing lights of red and blue, exploits the broken dream.

Handcuffs, handcuffs, shiny steel and power. Pivot slick and strong.
Click, click, unfold; fold, click. The damage has been done.
That young man couldn't escape your rage, now a man is dead.
You said it wasn't at all your fault, but your tires had no tread.

WHEN THE BOUGH BREAKS

Rock-a-bye baby on the treetop. When the wind blows, the
cradle will rock. Now don't put babies up in the trees. It's not a
good way to get them their Z's.
If the bough breaks, the cradle will fall, and that won't help
baby at all. Try a rock cliff, a crag, or precipice. Be baby
extreme. Not like the rest of us.
Teach him to fly, like birds on the wing. Give him a shove.
It's no big thing. He'll flap both his arms, though he doesn't
know why. Before he hits bottom, he'll know how to fly.
When he's learned it all well and flies from your lap, it's time
for the rocket, to strap on his back. Baby will fly, but boy must
go fast. He needs the extra power, for the sky is so vast.
He flies to and fro, now all feathered are his wings. You
watched him well; you helped him grow. Such thoughtful things.
He's so much a bird, now looking for Z's. On that small branch,
he'll perch.
You didn't teach him to stay out of the trees.

FAULTY REFLECTIONS

REFLECTIONS SOUGHT; GOOD MEMORIES THEY ARE NOT. THE MIRROR OF MY PAST
SHOWS ME THE REFLECTION I SEE IN THE MIRROR TODAY. I DO NOT WANT TO SEE IT
BUT I CAN NOT LOOK AWAY.
THE SOUND IS NOT, FOR MY MEMORY WILL NOT RETRIEVE THAT WHICH MY MIND HAS
DELETED. MUSICAL REMINDERS OF A PAINFUL PAST; REFLECTIONS OF PROJECTIONS
FROM THE OUTSIDE LOOKING IN AT ME.
COULD IT BE, THE REFLECTIONS I SEE WERE IMAGINED ABOUT ME, WITHOUT ME?
THERE IS A SPECTER I CAN NOT QUITE RETRIEVE BUT I THINK IT IS GOOD. CLARITY AND
MAYBE PEACE, IF ONLY I COULD. MEMORIES I WOULD LIKE TO SEE; MEMORIES THAT
WANT TO BE.

BUT THE MUSIC BOX IS EMPTY.

A BEAUTIFUL DAY

I'm so sorry.
It won't get above 50° today. We'll have 48% humidity and partly cloudy skies.
We'll have windy conditions most of the day; with gusts up to 8 mph. But don't worry it'll be better tomorrow!
It's a beautiful day today!
It's already 81° on its' way to a high of 97°! There will be absolutely no moisture in the air, not a cloud to be seen, and no wind at all! Like I said; a beautiful day!
Make sure your AC is working well and your house is well insulated with thick reflective window coverings. Don't leave your children or pets in your car for more than 2½ minutes; even with your windows rolled down slightly, you could still fry an egg on the dashboard. After 10 minutes it will be 112°; 20 minutes-120° and after 28 minutes it will be 130°.
Don't forget to put on your UV-A, UV-B AND UV-C with SPF 100 sun block. Put on your UV 400 sun glasses and a wide brim lite color summer hat. Try not to drive at sunrise, noon or sunset; many accidents are caused by drivers being temporarily blinded by the glare.
You'll want to wear light clothing. Don't forget to wear shoes; sidewalks and asphalt will give you 2nd degree burns; even sand could give you blisters.
If you're planning outdoor activities try to get it done before 7:30am.
A swim would be good if the neighborhood pool is not too crowded.
Maybe you should just stay home, with the AC cranked up and enjoy this great day from the inside.

LOST AND FOUND

As time goes by, we often look
At all the things we left and took
Took are the things we're going to keep
Left are the things that made us weep
It is in these things in which we wept
We often find the things we kept

WELCOME HOME

Glad you're out; it's been a long time
I'm sorry about your family
But you're not alone
And you have a place to stay
I know what you did
But I know who you are
And I'll always be your friend
Welcome home man

CLOUDS OF DESIRE

The softness of your touch has taken on a whole new feel. A pleasure
only in my dreams until this night. Maybe our parents are right.
As I give myself to you, know you that I am in control.
Tension fades, adrenalin rises. You can feel the heat between us.
The friction goes as the steam begins to rise. The chill is gone and
the night becomes a blur.
I command your soul, at least for now, and you give in with ease.
So take my hand, embrace my lips and surrender.
The night is ours. Alone, but not lonely, we fall together and dream
of love, love not yet felt in spirit, but for now the flesh will do.
Though it is not true, speak of your love for me. You'll find the words
will soothe us both.
The passion in your eyes tempts my surrender, but I must stay in control.
You are mine for the night, and the night is ours. Our passion will not be
quelled, for our desire is strong and true.
We will travel the night and find blissful surrender in the clouds
of desire.
As we become one, we will explore uncharted ground, and never forget
our glance at love.

FOOD CHAIN

If I had a conscience, I would stalk you and only watch,
but that's not my nature.
Your grace, speed and beauty are to be respected,
still to respect is not my place.
You're so aware of all that is around you; yet, still you
don't know I'm here. I've been watching you now for
several hours; waiting for my time to pounce.
Your beauty I find intoxicating; so intense in my tunnel
vision; so pure is my intent for you, and adrenaline
sharpens the edge.
It's hard to stay in control, when you're so close I can
nearly touch you.
If I move too fast, you might get away; I will have
wasted all that time.
The chase is fun, but it means nothing without the kill.
I'll just be patient a little while more. It's what I do and
I'm good at it.
I know you've never done anything to me; you're
innocent, clean and pure.
My hunger though is all I know. I'm gonna do what I do.
It's the nature of things.
      And you're food on my chain.

THE TRAVELER YOU CAN'T KNOW

You have no friends, and your enemies meet death before you leave them. Once respect would follow you; now it precedes you. You have become known to most, yet no one knows your name.

Remaining constant, the company of your weapon and armor with you always, you are not alone. Cleaned and polished so death will only be met on your terms.
You are ready but not willing; it is not your time. There are: villages, women and kingdoms to be conquered, lives, spirits and hearts to be broken.
Behind you: death, new life, love and lust, memories and new goals left waiting. Waiting are the faces that you only will remember.
You are hope for many, death for some, evil, or the devil to the shallow ones.
You love and leave, kill and tease. You won't be had, and you can't be followed.

*So what's next? Do you know? Does it matter? Tell me please.
Where will you go? Do you wait for a sign to show? Will you
go where the wind will blow?*

*I wish you would stay, though I know you cannot. I know that
I am but another conquest you have made, and you will leave
me, as you have done the rest.*

*There is only one way I can make you stay. I have gained your
trust, so from me you have nothing to fear.*

*I notice you a-top this rock, surveying the land below. I'm sorry
my love; it feels so wrong, but it's the only way I know to keep
you with me, to love no other. Now you can never go.*

The knife within your back is a symbol of my love.

*I take this symbol with your blood; I take my life and mix our
crimson past to be with you forever; an eternity above.*

Goodbye and hello, Traveler I don't know.

You Knew

You were around when I was accused and thought not much of it.
You knew how they came cunningly in the dark of the early morning
to take me away by force; and when they took me to the priest, you
witnessed my humiliation; then took me to the high priest for more.
My blood meant pain, and to come, much more; and you knew it.
Your governor tried me third and could not discern my guilt; so your
orders took me to the king, who desired me face to face; and when not
amused... back to the governor I went; and you led my parade to town.
The hate throughout the city against me was breathable but you had
yourself to think about.
You saw how I was treated and observed my resolve.
You heard the truth about me and it was hard to ignore but you were
"just doing your job".
Time after time I could have walked free but the hate chained my fate;
so you took me to the skull.
As I hung there bleeding and shamed, I breathed my last and you were
still there.
When darkness cut short the day and day became night: the earth
shook, the thunder roared and lightning filled the sky.
You witnessed it all and couldn't help know, nor keep it to yourself.
Exclaiming it loud for all to hear;
SURELY THIS WAS THE SON OF GOD!

It's a dragon, it's a plane; it's a submarine in the sky;
A thousand miles an hour; Funny bunny rabbit, where is your tail?
Alligator wrestler; not doing so well. Dragster burn out;
A thousand miles an hour; slowly floating by.
Bright beam light, shining through the mist so bright.
Burning the water; a thousand miles an hour, 'till it is no more.

EXESTENTIAL ADMONITIONS

If two debate and one doesn't enjoy it,
It's not a debate. It's an argument.

Be careful how you judge others.
You know how easy it is to do wrong.

I say: you are what you say I am, so be careful your accusations.

Be careful of what mold you put yourself in or allow yourself to be put in.
When it solidifies, it can be very hard to break out of.

All those I know, I have made all known; still I go to heaven alone.

Remember when logic was common?
Let's bring it back; it just makes sense.

People today reject what God freely gave
and embrace that which satan constantly makes them pay for.

When doing nothing brings boredom, a different nothing can be exciting.

YOU CAN'T THINK AN UNTHINKABLE THOUGHT; THAT WOULD BE UNTHINKABLE?

Today is tomorrow if yesterday is today

If you're thinking about not thinking about it, you're thinking about it.

Shadows live

Have you ever felt like some-one was watching you but no-one was there?
Have you ever felt that you were in a room with several other people but you were alone?
Consider the shadow.
A person can have many shadows; one for every light source. Even low light can produce a
shadow.
I recently postulated the theory that human shadows actually have life.
Considering no-one has a constant shadow, there is no time for sentience to develop.
Even still it would likely take a few thousand years to achieve even the slightest awareness.

Photons; when passing through humans, lose their positive charge, and begin to spin in the
opposite direction. While not effected by gauge bosons they become a form of negative
dark antimatter particles (NDAPs) with less than zero mass. Even so... or should I say so,
the shadow appears.
These particles have an energy of their own; an energy we haven't been able to
quantify. Even our most sensitive instruments detect nothing.
Clearly though, without energy, shadows could not exist; they would lose all
symmetrical cohesion.
Even with the wave-particle dyad, an NDAP does not exhibit wave interference with itself.
This results in multiple finite and infinite properties at the same time. This phenomenon is only
visually tangible in this time frame. Though appearing to be spatially localized and in as much as
they appear to be two dimensional, I am certain that shadows actually exist in at least
four dimensions.
In this "shadow state", the NDAPs do not interact with electrons. This could only indicate
a fourth dimension. Though we can visually account for the shadow, it doesn't exist in our
time frame; but in a dimension only nanoseconds outside of our time.
Given the frequency dependence of light energy, the matter of smoke or fog demonstrates
a third dimension and indicates a four dimensional effect as the NDAPs approach zero time.

In my professional opinion, the independent nature of NDAPs leaves no room for debate;
as they generate organized chaos while maintaining a thermal equilibrium. Only life can accomplish
such wonderful contradictory valence; the smoke and fog models demonstrate this direction of
propagation. Therefore in the declaration of this paradigm I maintain and proclaim to the world; our
shadows live.

KEEPING AMERICA FREE

When I write home and explain
what I do over here,
 They don't understand.
But they know I defend our land
 And keep America free.
That's good enough for me.

NO NOEL

As the dawn became anew
And the sun began to rise
I knew that I knew that I knew
That Santa had passed me by

I tried to keep hope
That I was just the last stop
That still he might show
And fill up my sock

The Christmas lights were on
They glowed all through the night
I sat out the cookies and milk
I know I did everything right

I shouldn't have stayed up late
That's what I did wrong
I should've went to sleep early
Like it says to in the song

My eye-lids were getting heavy
I think I went to sleep
I was slipping into dream land
And my sleep was getting deep

I could see my family around me
Though my eyes were still tight shut
"Bobby you're missing Christmas"
But they could not wake me up

The next thing I remember
Is what my parents always said
On the 24th of December
You must early go to bed

I knew by now I'd missed it
And Santa I would not see
"Wake up Bobby it's Christmas"
Well I guess it was just a dream

It's really Christmas morning
I thank you God a lot
Thank you for baby Jesus
And that Santa has filled my sock

LET LOOSE THE RATS OF WAR

It's funny how one pet rat can turn into so many so fast. It seemed to us that Ben needed
companionship. So we got him a girlfriend. After a few weeks we found eleven tiny pink babies.
In a few months we had a small army with every color and style you could imagine.
My brother and me had seen the movie "Willard" and decided that we could train our rats too.
Turns out that we could. Our rats knew their names. They understood the words no and food.
They would come when we called and would stand on their hind legs on command. They could walk
a tight rope or a loose one for that matter. They could do all kinds of tricks and would stay on our
shoulders when we went for a bike ride. They were very friendly to us and we loved them very
much.
Our parents didn't think any more of the rats than they did our friends and that's not saying much.
I can't tell you how many times dad threatened to pinch their heads off if he saw one loose in the
house one more time. They never really caused any trouble and the fact is they were out a lot more
than dad thought. They all knew when to stay out of sight and who to hide from.

One day without asking me or my brother, the folks let us know we were moving to another state.
They knew we wouldn't want to leave, so they decided without us.
We had a lot of good friends and loved our home. We even liked our school.
As if leaving behind so much wasn't enough, they told us that we couldn't take any of the rats.
I don't think they understood exactly what they were saying or how much our pets meant to us.
They were family just like our dog and they would never leave her behind.
Of course, we let our parents know exactly how we felt but it couldn't have meant less to them.
No matter how much we begged them to call off the move or at least let the rats go with us, they just
ignored us and went on with their moving plans. I guess they just weren't thinking about what plans
we might have.
They could've tried to be cool and work with us. We might have been ok with just a few rats going
with us but they didn't even try. They didn't care. THIS WAS WAR!
Before long the house was for sale and people were coming in and looking around.
It was easy to hide the empty cages in our closets so the lookyloos had no idea we had pet rats and
our parents didn't know what we were up to.
It's amazing how over sixty rats could stay so well hidden.
One day a nice young couple looked very interested. It seemed to be all over and not one rat to be
seen (like I said they knew when to hide). The couple said they wanted to come back one more time
to decide. We needed a new strategy.
We knew our rats could chew through anything, so I figured if we put some of mom's bacon grease
on a few wires and pipes and maybe a small corner somewhere strategic, we might still win this
war.
The night before the next meeting we let loose the rats and pointed them in the right direction. It
was just so easy! Oh yeah, don't worry, the wires we chose were not live (at the time).
The next day all rats were accounted for (as far as we could tell) and everything was in its place.

Our parents were very excited and figured this was the one. The young couple seemed to have already made up their mind so it didn't seem to bother them too much when the garage door didn't open. None of the dining room lights would work and the minor flood coming from under the kitchen sink (almost) looked like something chewed through the pipe. They figured these were easy fixes and were about to sign the papers. It didn't look good! In my mind I could see my dad holding cages full of rats under the water until the bubbles stopped floating to the top.
The husband was about to sign the papers when the wife let out a scream that would've made a B movie actress jealous. She could've sworn she saw a pair of beady eyes looking out through a small hole in the living room wall next to the back sliding door.
The couple left and I could see smoke coming out of dad's ears. I think he knew what we did.

We were in our room waiting for our punishment to be handed down when dad rushed in like a crazy man yelling and freaking out. We took cover under the bed but when we peaked out from under, we could see he was actually happy and laughing.
 It turned out, he had just got a call from the company that was about to hire him to work in that other state. Apparently, the company decided not to open their facility in that state after all but would be starting business a few miles away and wanted dad to run the whole operation.

Now our parents ask our opinions about everything and they know all the main rat's names by heart. They also make sure that all the rats have nothing but the best food. They even smile when the rats show up at the dinner table to score on some table scraps.
It's funny how things work out.
Those were good days!

IN MEMORY OF:
BEN
CHASSY
BEN JR.
SOCRATES
SPIKE
BUZZ
WILLARD
TAURIAN
SCOOTER
SCOOTER JR.
KESS
WEEJIBOW
NOMAD

Take the top left and the bottom right – it is two.
Take the bottom left and the top right – it is five.
Take the bottom left and the top left – it is three.
Take the top right – it is six.
Leave the top right and the bottom right – it is one.
Leave it alone – it is eight.

A CLUE MARKED IN WATER

RIDDLED

Why is a Volkswagen bug, like an elephant?

Besides Adam and Eve who was the only person in the bible
with no parents at all?

What was the last thing Ananias and Sapphira said to Peter
when he asked if they really sold their land for so much?

If the USB is for the PC and the AV is for the DVD;
If STP is for the ATV and 10w30 for the SUV;
If the MVP is for the NFL;
What is PMS for?

Ye shall find no answers here.

                    Seek ye first the wet pages.

TWISTED DESTINY

As I sit atop this manmade wonder, I think way back to my
childhood days. I remember so much, yet so little was good.
Still, I'd like to go back in so many ways.
I used to look up and stare at the wonder; at these man-made
towers that touch the sky.
My thoughts would run rampant, and I'd always see death;
many dead people, but I didn't know why.

Now I'm on top and looking down. So many people, and
none of them know. They don't know I'm here. No-one
suspects. They'll all be a part of my farewell show.

I've got all my props; I'm ready for action. I'll be famous soon,
and that is for certain. I open up with joy, and watch the ants fall.
There'll be many more before the last curtain.

I've got the lead role, yet nobody knows me. But I'll be big
soon; a household name.
The ants keep falling, only fewer now. It still doesn't bug me,
they all look the same.

The streets are clear now; only dead ants remain. Except for
the blue ants that want me dead.
There's a rap at the door; the one that I locked. It won't be
long now. Again I see red.
The door breaks open. Someone calls out… it's all over now.
Lay down your arms.
It's all been too easy. It's just what I want. I jump in the open;
I'm joining the stars.
As I breathe my last breath, the last thing I hear…
Who is he anyway…? The answer I feared…

Nobody knows

NEIGHBORS

I once asked a neighbor couple if my music was too loud. They said: "no we never hear anything coming from your apartment; besides we like the tunes you've been playing".
I thought that was pretty funny.

I have a neighbor on the first floor (I'm on the third floor) that has been here since I moved in. Turns out he was a loud techno "music" subwoofer "dance" party kind of a guy. I usually couldn't hear the "music" but the subwoofer drove me nuts.
I went down stairs, friendly beer offering in hand to ask if he would just turn off the subwoofer; not to worry about the music.
He wouldn't take the beer and didn't invite me in, but said he would turn it down.
I don't know if he even touched the knob.
After a few years of trying to respectfully get him to stop the sub-sonic misery, I gave up.
A few years later he started cranking his subwoofer so loud, the entire building would shake, and since his window and door were open the whole neighborhood could share in the misery.
One day I couldn't put up with it anymore. I went outside and yelled downstairs for him to stop it. He yelled back at me, and said: he would turn off the subwoofer if I would turn off my air conditioner.
 (I didn't make him move into an apartment with three ac. units not far from his window.)
I told him he could turn up his music to cover the noise, just please not the subwoofer. His answer…
If your ac. comes on, the subwoofer comes on.
How do you communicate with someone that reasons in such a bizarre manner? I've met five-year-olds with more respect and reason than that!

I asked a new neighbor if he could give my car a jump; he grabbed his cables and pulled his car up next to mine. We hooked up the cables and let my car start charging. While the car was getting juiced, I asked how he was liking his new home and that started a conversation. Turns out he was a pretty nice guy and we got along great. After a while I tried the car and it started just fine.
"Well," he said: "I've got to get back home; I'll talk to you later". I put a look of sad fear on my face and said: "Noooo I want to talk" (like a little kid that didn't want to go to bed). You should have seen the look on his face. I don't believe I have ever noticed such a look on a man's face before. It was hilarious.
With his look of surprised confusion, he started to get in his car as I tried to explain about my sense of humor. He hasn't had much to say to me since then.

IT'S A DIGITAL THING

I'LL SEE YOU THERE DAD

WHEN I WAS A BOY, DAD TOLD ME IF I WANT TO WIN A BICYCLE RACE, I'VE GOT TO KEEP
THE BIKE STRAIGHT AND NOT WOBLE BACK AND FORTH; THAT ONLY WASTES ENERGY.
HE ALSO TOLD ME IF I'M RUNNING IN A FOOT RACE TO NOT LOOK BACK; THAT ONLY
WASTES ENERY AND TAKES YOUR EYES OFF THE GOAL.
I DIDN'T REALIZE AT THE TIME, THE DEEPER MEANING THAT HIS WORDS CARRIED BUT
NOW, I THINK I'LL RUN THE RACE UPRIGHT, FOCUSED ON THE GOAL AND NOT WASTE
TIME AND ENERGY LOOKING BACK AT WHAT WAS OR MIGHT BE.
OH YEAH HE ALSO TOLD ME TO CUT MY HAIR...
WELL I GOT TWO OUT OF THREE.

I KNOW THAT IF DAD COULD HAVE GOD SEND US AN ANGEL WITH A MESSAGE, HE WOULD
TELL US TO BE HAPPY FOR HIM AND CELEBRATE HIS MEMORY AND THE JOY OF HIS NEW LIFE
IN PARADISE; FOR-EVER.
AND I KNOW DAD HAS A SPECIAL MESSAGE FOR GREG;

"THANK YOU SON FOR SHOWING ME THE WAY!"

I ALSO BELIEVE HE WOULD TELL US; **"YOUR SISTER TANYA SAYS HELLO", AND, "I LOVE YOU GUYS".**

I LOVE MY DAD AND I LOOK FORWARD TO SEEING HIM IN HEAVEN AND HEARING HIM SAY
AT LEAST ONE MORE TIME;
"HI SON"!

THE SOUND OF PILLS

The bottle fills your hand perfect and it feels good because
you know what it means. You love the sound as it rattles
when you pick it up and take it to your bedroom.
Take off the cap; quiet rattle rapture: anticipation,
excitement, a little fear, and hope.
A pill in hand; it's not enough, two look better but I think
three; and whiskey sour sets the pace.
A man on a mission. It will happen; just let it be. This is not
a race. Still it's taking so long. It's hard to wait.
Try to relax but that's the point. More sour, a bigger glass.
More whiskey I think.
Another pill, maybe two or three but that should not be.
This isn't the plan. It's taking too long. Check the bottle.
What went wrong? It can't be expired. What did you do?
You're not even tired... You drunken fool...
"What is Pamprin?"
Shock, dismay; mind in disarray what have you done?
Pills on the floor; a sound not heard before.
Everything is worse; your mind is not stable. I guess you
can't read a simple label.
And no I don't want to talk about your feelings now.

MONKEY ON MY BACK

There's a monkey on my back, and I can't get him off. He won't
let me be and it's making me weary.
I'm still the same person that I've always been, yet my friends
don't see it; they act so leery.
I try so hard, yet to no avail. This monkey's too tough, and it's
making me weak.
I've had troubles before, but I was always on top. Now friends
shy away. My life's looking bleak.
My woman gets jealous; she don't understand. I've tried to
explain; it's the law of the land. Once you get started, they won't
let you be. I thought I could stop it. Now it's too much to stand.
Even little boy just don't understand. I tried to explain, but he
said I look silly.
I've said I could stop this; there must be a way. My friends keep
laughing.
But I know I can; really!
Now it's all so clear. Potassium will do it. I should have thought
of it sooner, and I know where to find some.
It's almost all over; I'll be on top once again. Once I give what
he's wanted, I will have won.
It's a jungle out there; it's a fight every day. But I'm one of a
kind; I'm a special man.
Now I'm back on top; king of all I survey.
I'm the king of the jungle. They call me Tarzan.

You hurt my feelings so I hurt you. If I have to feel bad it's only fair
that you do too.
How else can this problem be solved? How else to be satisfied?
Hurt me hurt you. I've gotta get even, but you do too.
What comes around goes around, and when it comes again,
I'll be ready to make it worse... and if you hurt me back,
I'll hurt you even more. If you ask me to stop, I'll show you the door,
and slam it on your hand.
You can't win this; it's all I have.
If you give up, I win. If you don't, I win.
Like I said: this is all I have, and I can do it forever.

PHILOSOPHY; DEEP OR NOT

The wind will blow
so the rats can't see
The rock that fell
can now be free

It's no use standing
against brick walls
The Jell-O within
floods all empty halls

Sometimes people
don't care where they are
Young cats can't help
but watch from afar

Open doors get locked
when the sound is too low
The rats jump higher
yet deeper they go

All toads grin
at the sight of candy
Open mouths drool
'cause the kittens are handy

The harp yells out
for no one to hear
The orb spins on
but is it clear

If you understand
philosophy's strife
Read the words
Is it all about life

THE TRUNK IS IN FRONT

NEVER THE LESS

Never more, never less
Have some more, never the less
It's all too much, it's never enough
It always changes, never the less

Be all, be nothing
Never start, never stop
Going up, watch it drop
It stays the same, never the less

WHISTLER'S WALK

I'm not a bad man
My fate's not deserved
I'd love most to change it
And be the one served

But what can I do
In this strange land
Where black men are ruled
By the white man's hand

I cook all his meals
But what do I get
Maybe the leftovers
No not one bit

I don't get paid
When I do a good job
But if I make a mistake
I'll likely get flogged

I am not a thief
I don't like to steal
It still wouldn't matter
The path would reveal

If I tasted his food
He'd know right away
He would hear no whistle
This black man would pay

So for the rest of my days
Like my father before me
I'll serve the white man
'Till I become free

He won't let me go
But I'm not discouraged
I'll be free one day
With the last of my courage

I can't fight my foe
But there's something I can do
The meal I prepared
I'll consider my own food

I'll eat all I like
As I walk down that path
The white man will know
And he'll show me his wrath

I know what will happen
But it's my time to steal
The whistler's walk
Will be my last meal

GET OFF MY BACK

Get off my back little snail. You can make it on your own.
You may think I live in the fast lane, but I really take it slow.
You decided that you're bored, and need to make a change,
but speeding up is not the answer. Just take it slow, the way
you know, you're already equipped for that.
The rest of the world sees me slow, but they don't see you at all.
Take advantage of this wonderful gift; it's an advantage you can
use.

Most of the world moving swiftly; passing so much as they go.
Missing the world that's all around them, and they don't even
know.

I'm happy to say I move slowly and see much more than most.
You can see much more than I. So why follow me?
Life is too short to move so fast; to get to there and back. Take
your time, enjoy the trip, poke your head out, and look at the
world around you.
Be happy with the way you are. Enjoy your little world.
You don't need to be seen and get attention. What good
would that really do?

Be seen and take your chances. Be swift and lose control.
Live your life by using me; see the dangers there can be,
when it's my time to feed…You'll float on top when I submerge;
then you're food.
Maybe you should get off my back now, before I get to the lake.

WHAT IF 6 WERE 9

**IF 6 WERE 9 I'D BE UPSIDE DOWN AND TURNED AROUND
GRAVITY WOULD FALL UP AND SMOKE WOULD RISE DOWN
E WOULD BE 3... L-7...M-W... BUT ALL IS NOT LOST; H IS STILL H
AND I IS I... O-O AND X-X. BUT WHAT IF 9 TURNED OUT TO BE 6?**

YOU'RE IN TOO DEEP

Sink deep into the darkness at the bottom of your glass. This is your last day on earth and you know it. You'll never now see the light of day. You're in too deep; stuck in the cold mire of drunken despair. You'll get no older; the chill of death embraces you. But you can't cross over.
Sink into the deep where there is no light. Let go and sink; don't try to fight. That'll ruin everything. There's a plan for you in hell, but why go alone? There's still more time to share the dark.
Your fellow flotsam does not hide. It will embrace your charm as you make the darkness appeal.
Fill the pit like you fill your glass… thoughtless abandon plan. All filled up and empty; pouring out like flowing shards of ice in the vastness of encompassing death.
No victory. You were never in the fight. Your score zero. It would be better if you had never been.

JOSHUA 1:1

MY TRAIN

Train run over me; Make it loud; Sweet locomotive breeze.
Heavy iron horse; My time; Its' rage; Ear splitting thunder
beneath this rail and tie cage.
This cage is not all mine; I thought I'd share it with you. You
dared me to lie beneath the track, so I thought you should too.
Cowardly hypocrite little boy; You thought you'd have some
fun.
Now the train is coming and it's too late for you to run.
Feel the breeze; Hear the thunder; Your time; Its' rage; Can't
hear your screams from this rail and tie cage. Stop your crying;
this was your notion. You said it would be fun, so why all the
emotion? I think it was more fun than you planned; to put me in
my place; to be or not a man.
Have you another test in mind? Another inward truth to find?
Dare you dare me, your participation is required.

TELLING TELLING TOLD

Teller, teller, tell me some more
Make it sound real, make the words soar
Push it in my brain; tell me that it's serious
Redundant words abound, 'till my mind swims delirious

Teller, teller, tell me the telling
Make it sound deep, keep my small mind swelling
Fill me overflowing; tell me that it's new
When the telling is told 'till I'm deeper than you
I'll tell the told tellings
Now I'm a teller too

I love my family; taking care of them and the home
is a very rewarding job. It's just, once Bill is off to work
and the kids are at school there is only so much I can do.
Because I keep up with the chores daily, I finish early;
leaving nothing to do but sit alone and watch the television.
One day I was watching a program that focused on a
village in a foreign country where the women had to beg,
pick trash or prostitute themselves. Most of them involved
in the latter; some by choice, some not.
It was breaking my heart and I couldn't watch anymore,
so I turned the television off and sat there trying to think
of something to do. A hobby; a part time job; something.
I'm a pretty good seamstress and I love fashion but there
is no need for such talents in this small town. I need to do
something. I need to feel useful; to make a difference.
As I sat there pouting, I thought how the women in that
story needed to be useful in a much more desperate
manner. It all seemed hopeless.
Then... inspiration from God. I could design and teach.
I called a friend with similar talents and invited her over
for coffee.
She was as excited as me. We decided we had to start
small but we still needed money, cooperation from our
men and a lot of patience from our kids.

It turned out they were proud of us and wanted to help;
so Bill turned the computer on and started a web page to
solicit funds for travel and material.
Before long, thanks to a lot of generous people we had
more than we could have hoped.
So here we are with these beautiful women; making hand
bags and pretty dresses; each with her own special touch.
They can't stop smiling and telling us how happy they are
to not have to beg, pick trash or stand in that shameful
line.
Tears fill my eyes with joy as I watch happy women and
 colorful fashion fill the streets of this little village.
Now I'm making a big difference; these women are very
useful and women all over the world are using these
custom bags and wearing the beautiful dresses; handmade
by these gorgeous ladies.

Crime is way down: the town is becoming prosperous,
children play in clean streets and people are smiling.
My heart is full and my family couldn't be more proud.

FRAGILE AS AN EGG

Your heart is as fragile as an egg; in fact, it's who you are.
Your heart is what you're about; it's the wellspring of life;
covered in this fragile shell that you see is who you are.
Is this shell more important to you than what comes after?
Would you rip out your heart as a convenience? Is today's
convenience more important than tomorrow's joy?
What about the joy still to come?
The decisions you make are important; they're what makes
next happen. If you destroy life, no one can put it back together,
and there will be no next.
You avoid war at all cost. You stay in the shade to protect that
fragile shell. You don't play with fire and you stay out of the
boiling water.
        So why do you sit on the wall?

<u>ARE WE THERE YET</u>

WAKE UP, GET UP, TIME'S A WASTIN', WE'RE BURNIN' DAYLIGHT.
WE'VE GOTTA GET ON THE ROAD AND BEAT THE TRAFFIC.
 GET A MOVE ON; LET'S GO!
Do we gotta? Can't we leave after the traffic?
DON'T TALK BACK; DO AS I SAY.

IS EVERYTHING PACKED? ARE WE READY TO GO...?
OK WE'RE OFF.
Honey, wait; I think I left the stove on. I'll be right back.

NOW, IF NO-ONE FORGOT ANYTHING ELSE WE'LL GET MOVIN.'

Daddy Taylor touched me
Well he touched me first.
STRAIGHTEN UP OR I'LL TURN THIS CAR AROUND.
Good, I can go back to sleep.
Noo Taylor; I want to see Mighty Mouse.
YOU TELL HIM JANEY. WE CAN SLEEP ANY TIME.

FIRST PIT STOP; ALL OUT THAT'S GOING OUT. WE WON'T
BE STOPPING FOR A WHILE. TAKE CARE OF YOUR BUSINESS NOW.

WE'RE A LITTLE BEHIND SCHEDULE DEAR. SEE IF YOU CAN FIND
 US A SHORT CUT TO THE NEXT TOWN.
*Exit 105, 2 miles, then right at the first light. That should take
us directly there.*
THIS IS BENNET NOT STILLWELL. NOW WE'RE 78 MILES IN
THE WRONG DIRECTION. WE WERE BETTER OFF BEFORE.
Well then, don't ask me for directions anymore; do it yourself.

Are we there yet?
No, sit down and behave.

Honey, did you hear a noise?
NO, IT'S JUST YOUR IMAGINATION.

I'm hungry.
EAT THE LUNCH YOUR MOTHER FIXED YOU.
But I don't like tuna.
Then eat the bologna.
Taylor ate the bologna. I'm hungry.
YOU WON'T STARVE; YOU CAN EAT WHEN WE GET THERE.
But daaad...
DON'T MAKE ME COME BACK THERE.

WILL YOU HAND ME A CIGARETTE PLEASE DEAR?
Hey dad I want one too.
NO. SMOKING IS BAD FOR YOU.
Well... you do it.
IF I JUMPED OFF A BRIDGE, WOULD YOU JUMP OFF THE BRIDGE TOO?
I would if I had a parachute.
JUST DO AS I SAY, NOT AS I DO.

Are we there yet?
YES, NOW STOP YOUR WHINING.
No, we're not; there's nothing anywhere around here.
THEN WHY DID YOU ASK?
I don't know.
TREY, GO SIT IN THE BACK.
Why?
BECAUSE I SAID SO.
But...
*Listen to your father and be quiet. He's too busy to argue
with you kids.*

Daad, Taylor said I'm adopted.
TAYLOR DON'T TELL YOUR SISTER SHE'S ADOPTED.
But I didn't.
DON'T ARGUE; JUST KEEP QUIET.

OK, WE'RE HERE; EVERYBODY PILE OUT.
quiet… the kids are asleep; you'll wake them up.
Honey, why is the parking lot so empty?
I DON'T KNOW. IT MUST BE A SLOW DAY. I'LL GO TO THE TICKET
OFFICE AND GET OUR PASSES, WHILE YOU WAKE UP THE KIDS.

WE APOLOGIZE FOR THE INCONVENIENCE
WE WILL BE CLOSED ALL MONTH FOR
REPAIRS AND NEW RIDES
WE'LL SEE YOU NEXT MONTH

@#%@#*%!*?@#! DAGG-NABBIT

GET IN THE CAR AND LET'S GO.
I told you they would be closed this month,
but you wouldn't listen…
NOT ANOTHER WORD!
                    Are we there yet?

FLY BEATNIK

I CANNOT FLY;
I AM NOT A FLY.
I DON'T KNOW WHY.
A FLY CAN FLY.
I AM NOT A FLY.
FLY, FLY; FLY.

THE EVE OF ALL HALLOWS

The sun begins to sink
As it touches the mountain peaks
Orange red and black fills the night sky
as the howling wind brings distant shrieks

All kinds of strange little creatures
scampering in the shadows
Their goal to reap the riches
for it is the eve of all hallows

Spiders, rats, and witches; all the night walking
Scary furry faces at every front door
Lonely people waiting for that bell to ring
Little greedy creatures eager for what's in store

Charlie, Lucy and Linus waiting for the great pumpkin to appear
Chuck and Lucy cringe from a howling so near
Linus laughing at their childish fear
It is only that loner Snoopy you hear

It's a holiday celebration
for the morbid and weird
Goblins, zombies and monsters
But they're not to be feared

It's a game for the young
still adults like to play
It's hours of fun
till the light brings the day

It's all over now
And it's been a lot of fun
We'll have to wait another year
for the little monsters to come

UNDYING LOVE

I DREAM OF JEANNIE
WITH THE JET BLACK HAIR
HER LEGS ARE LONG AND PERFECT
AND HER SKIN IS RATHER FAIR

HER BODY FILLS HER DRESS
LIKE A HAND SHOULD FIT A GLOVE
HER FACE IS DOWNRIGHT GORGEOUS
I THINK I AM IN LOVE

YOU'D NEVER KNOW SHE'S PURE
AND GOES TO CHURCH ON SUNDAY
SHE'S ALWAYS DRESSED IN BLACK
SHE'S THE DEVIL'S CHILD YOU'D SAY

HER EYES ARE RED AND BLACK
AS BEST AS I CAN TELL
SHE ALWAYS SPEAKS OF LOVE
SHE CANNOT BE FROM HELL

THE DEVIL WOULD BE HAPPY
TO HAVE THIS GIRL OF MINE
BUT THAT WILL NEVER HAPPEN
FOR SHE STAYS WITHIN MY MIND

I'LL BET YOU ALL YOUR MONEY
THERE ISN'T SUCH A GIRL
BUT IF THERE WERE - TO FIND HER
I'D TRAVEL 'ROUND THE WORLD

MY MIND IS FILLED WITH LUST
AS I WRITE THIS DOWN ON PAPER
NOW THE DRUGS ARE WEARING OFF
I HOPE THAT I CAN SAVOR

THESE FEELINGS THAT I'VE GOT
THE PICTURES IN MY MIND
IF ONLY I COULD REMEMBER
HOW MANY DRUGS AND WHAT KIND

I'D NEVER LEAVE MY TRUE LOVE
SHE'D BE WITH ME ALL MY LIFE
IF THE DRUGS WOULD NEVER RUN OUT
I'D MAKE THIS GIRL MY WIFE

I KNOW THAT SHE'S NOT REAL
BUT MY LOVE WILL NEVER DIE
MY LOVE WILL ALWAYS BE THERE
AS LONG AS I AM HIGH

THE REAL REAL

This reality is more real than any reality you've ever
imagined
It doesn't require your imagination because it's the real
reality.
It doesn't matter what you think or how you feel, it still is
and that won't change.
You ask: "If I tell you 2+2=3; who are you to tell me I'm
wrong"?
Clearly you live in a different reality; one that exists only in
the minds of the most empty-headed sheep-monkeys in this
world. You have to be taught to be that kind of stupid.
Monkey see monkey do, follow the sheep in front of you.
Can't you even try to think for yourself?
I don't believe that your pin head has the cranial capacity to
hold enough grey matter to comprehend the fact of true
reality and I know you don't understand what I just said; so I
won't try to explain.
The fact of the matter is, real is real and the vast majority of
humans understand the real reality, no matter what your god
(TV) says.
It doesn't matter what you think or how you feel, real is real
and that won't change.
My recommendation to you is: go sit down in your parents'
basement:
play video games,
eat pizza,
get fat
and fade away.

Good riddance you dim-witted sheep monkey.

IF I'M LIE'IN I'M DIE'IN

Acts 5:1-10

HAPPY BIRTHDAY FAYE

Happy birthday, happy birthday; this is your day.
Twenty nine again and so many more to come.
Young forever and then, forever home.
You are loved more than you could know.
Your life has brought forth so much good:
Two great sons and "Sonny" too...,
You are a valued friend and like a second mom.
I would never try to imagine life without you in it.
Keep up the good work and don't change a thing.

HAPPY BIRTHDAY FAYE
HAPPY BIRTHDAY TO YOU
HAPPY BIRTHDAY FAYE
KEEP DOING WHAT YOU DO

HAPPY BIRTHDAY!

OVERCOME

Deny thee not thine trepidations. Cast thee out not thine fears, lest ye embrace that which thou hast so fervently tried to deny. Embrace that, which thou hast so timidly proclaimed before man, that thou mightest learn, grow and overcome the defeated foe.

Thank you Heavenly Father for this food we're about to eat.
Thank you for blessing this food that it does us all good
and no harm. To make sure we're never anything you don't
want us to be but always what you do: healthy and strong
Lord, inside and out: body, mind, spirit and flesh.
We thank you God for giving us: strength, courage, boldness, intelligence, a
strong mind, wisdom and discernment.
Make us always best able and ready to serve you.
Help us Lord this day to put a smile on your face and certainly
not to grieve you. Amen.

GOD RIDES A HARLEY

It was cold when I started out and that was ok; I've been riding a long time;
I know how to stay warm. Just because it was 25° out didn't mean that I was
going to miss my job interview, but I did decide to wear a helmet for the warmth
(bad idea) (you'll see why in a minute).
Aside from the distracting noise of the wind blowing through the helmet, it was a
great ride (no, it's not the reason but it's a good one). I've never really been very
concerned about the weather, though I won't ride if it's too hot to wear my leather.
As long as there's no ice on the road, I'm cool… (Sorry).
I was the only one there not wearing a pink or baby blue sweater and drive there in
a new SUV. I sat down anyway. (You never know, maybe these guys were not
indicative of the company itself).
Well I didn't get the job; go figure. You would think they would want a man that wanted
the job bad enough to ride a motorcycle thirty five miles in the freezing damp cold just
for an interview. I guess they just weren't looking at it that way.
When I walked outside, I could see that it had been snowing for a while. I wiped the
snow from my seat: flipped the petcock, turned the key, pressed the starter and she
came to life. The road wasn't iced yet but the snow was wet and heavy. To be honest,
I like to ride in the snow - but this time I was wearing a helmet. I hadn't ever had trouble
with water from rain or snow getting inside my goggles but somehow water was dripping
from the rim of the helmet and doing that very thing. The goggles fogged up pretty bad.
It was getting hard to see, so I lifted my goggles and got my eyes blasted from cars and trucks
kicking up wet gravel and the snow itself (I'll never do that again). With my goggles
back on I couldn't see much. It was a miserable ride.
By this time I was close to the last off ramp and one main road home. The thing is,
it was a bad pot hole stretch of road. Even on a clear day I wouldn't be able to negotiate
that road without hitting at least a few holes, but this wasn't a clear day; it was cloudy dark
with a wall of snow and I only had one small triangle shaped spot in one side of my goggles
that I could see through. If my goggles were clear, this would be a rough ride but I could
barely see at all.
They say that God rides a Harley… well I believe it because I hit not one pot hole on
that entire road.
One right turn and a quick left and I'd be home.
The store is only five or six miles up the road and I think I'm running low on peanuts.
(Like I said: I like riding in the snow).

A DAY IN THE PAST

The sun beats down through a hazy red sky. Steam from the swamp brings a morning mist upon the earth. A strange eerie cry cuts through the usual sounds of the immediate habitat. A thunderous roar follows and repeats, as does the eerie cry. A faint, rapid, yet erratic pounding slowly reaches the ear. As it gets louder and eyes turn in the direction of the thunder, movement can be seen through the mist.
The rumble overcomes, and a creature of tremendous size thunders past; larger than life, but fearing death.
The creature has past, but the thunder gets closer. All sounds of life before have stifled in wake of the thunder past and coming. The coming thunder is as loud or more, faster yet not as erratic. A taller creature thunders past, echoing a chilling roar through the swamp.
Seconds later, the thunder stops, as does the cry.
One last roar as the dust begins to settle. A whimper as if one last gasp for life… then quiet.
Sounds before return.
It's peaceful now in this range of view. Yet just beyond sight an even more immense creature falls to the might of the same threat, as his brother watches. Concerned yet at ease in the safety of the deeper swamp, he and the rest return to their one goal in life. They duck their heads beneath the water, cultivate the swamp floor and survive, while watching other small creatures jumping from the water in fear of a different thunder; in a different world; on this planet long ago; they look away. Never to make the connection. Never to care.

GROW UP AND ROCK

62

I liked your music when you had long hair. Now you've matured and cut your hair short.
The music no longer rocks and only children listen to your songs.
It did work then, it would work now, but you matured for the sake of the kiddies.
What do you say to those of us that still like the rock?
I guess money talks louder, and integrity can go to hell.

Maybe someday you WILL mature and play MUSIC again for us adults.

IS

WHAT IS, IS WHAT IS AND ALWAYS HAS BEEN; BUT WHAT IS WAS WILL
NEVER BE AGAIN.
WHAT IS REMAINS UNTIL WHAT IS WAS; SO WHAT IS, IS NO LONGER.
WHAT IS WAS CAN'T BE AGAIN; FOR WHAT IS WAS ISN'T, IT IS.
WHAT IS WON'T BE; BECAUSE WHAT IS WOULD BE WHAT IS WAS.

SO WHAT IS WAS CAN'T BE WHAT IS IS WHEN WHAT IS WAS BECOMES
WHAT IS WILL BE.
IT IS WHAT IT IS; ISN'T IT?

*It's hard to believe such a thing could really happen.
The whole event was a nightmare, in the strictest meaning
of the word. She was like nothing I had ever seen.
I should have left when I had the chance, but something
about the girl made me second guess, deny, and reason
the unreasonable.
Her tales of woe; her parent's recent tragic death, and
her story of being left with no one. Her need for company:
love and family. Her repeated reference of being the last
of her kind.
Still… my eyes could see, but I was blind.
She could do no wrong. Her innocence and ambivalence of
the world around her, made her incapable of evil.
From the very first day she captivated my spirit,
heart and soul.
My spirit was on high. Now my heart and spirit have been
broken.
My soul will surely be damned; damned for allowing this
thing to continue.
My discovery of yesterday has forced my eyes open. I cannot
help now, but to see the truth; the truth of this creature that
I have come to call my wife. Too late now, my eyes are open.
The tragic death of her parents was the giving of life to their
child. If I had only known the truth before, I would not
have given her children. Now the deed done; too late to take
it back, I must give in. For I cannot kill that which I have
given life. Nor can I take away the breath of my wife.*

How could I have been so blind? How can I keep alive this would be dead race? I suppose I deserve it. It's entirely my fault. If I could only die before they come; if I could get away, I'd run. To no avail, my thoughts won't help.

My meal this night, to be my last. Though not for me; to bring to close my family's fast. I'll be devoured and watch me die. My children will feast. My wife will taste. She'll chew me up, in front of my eyes. She'll lick her lips and kiss me goodbye.

How tragic and awful to see, hear and feel yourself being eaten alive; so little at a time. How tragic indeed, to be eaten alive by your own family.

Lord forgive me for keeping alive a race of creatures that should have never been. Even worse, my eyes now open and opportunity at hand, I have not the ability within my heart to end this evil thing.

As I sit here in the silence of this empty cellar, I wait for them; wait for them to come for dinner.

I realize my mistake. The evil I have kept alive, and even made stronger.

My lack of action will undoubtedly mean the death of countless others.

To them I would beg forgiveness, for come dinner time, I will know the intenseness of the agony they will suffer. Only for me there will be an added pain; the pain of watching my own family devour my living flesh.

LAST ENTRY

Dinr has lasted 3 days now. I can not beliv Im still alive.
I should have bled to death or died from shock long ago.
NowI can no longer feel my legs for they are gone. I think I
have been in shock Sens the 1'st da I can only rember short
flashes. a grin on my sons face as he shars my thih with his
sister? my wife with alook of pride yet no soro for me.
My site and reson fading I can only

LAST ENTRY

I must have passed out I donot no wat day this is? It must
have been A whil for my lef arm is now gon. I cannot espress
my pane and agony` Still these words must be put down' It
is al I can do. I must give a chanc;; to whomever mit read
this.
This skrybe must survve. They will not destroy what they
cannot understd?
If someone reads this I hop it is soon. I hope these words wil
help to stop this evil,
Donot take this awful truth ligt. Bewar of the pail ones.
One could be Your wife!

Zed Venair

1642

It's so cool, staying home from school. There is so much to do
when you're home with the flu.
I have so many toys and so many games. I'll have so much fun.
I could stay home for days.
Mommy is worried about my cold. I think my brother never told.
My brother went to school today. I feel sorry for him.
I wonder what they're doing today in gym.
It's a lot of fun playing video games, but mommy said I must
stay in bed instead.
Maybe TV is a good thing to try, but daytime TV was not made
for me.
I wonder if Jeff and Brad and Tommy are at school. I guess
when they get home, they'll go swimming in Jeff's pool.
Two hours have passed, and I'm just bored silly.
"Mommy will you take me to school?
I feel a lot better, really!"

I DON'T KNOW

NEEDLE IN THE CAGE

Who would've left this here on the floor where anyone could see?
Someone might get the wrong idea of what happened here.
Take the needle out of the cage. We don't want anyone to think
we run that kind of reformatory.
Just because we house a bunch of animals here doesn't mean we
can't keep it clean.
When that gorilla Eddy recovers, clean him up and put him back in the cage.
He's still young; maybe when he gets back into his right mind, he'll
think about what he did. Maybe this time he learned his lesson.
I know he doesn't like it but when five strong men can't hold him, it's time
to put him down for a while.
If he'd stop taking candy from children, he'd have no candy to eat.
If he had no candy to eat, he would have no cavity to fill and we wouldn't
have to knock him out with drugs that make him feel so out of control.

I'll be checking on the monkey next. Sarah said he pick pocketed another
guest and stole some "NoDoze". We might have to pump his stomach again.
Tell the doc to prepare another syringe.

You stand there alone and depressed. The look in your eyes
makes me sad.
Your life has been rough; life has not come easy. Good things to
you have happened not. Depression is your life. Above you every
day, a cloudy sky looms.
I am not a knight in shiny armor, on horseback, riding to your
relief.
But I feel too. And when I look at you, my heart bleeds.
I would take your pain, if the ability was within me.
If only I could, I would cry for you.

SHEMO

Take SheMo. It Might Help with Some of your Symptoms.

Finally, you can go running through that wheat field you've been dreaming of.
Or, dangle your foot in a pond. Don't forget the long walk on the beach with the
love of your life… it'll happen…

SheMo could cause a rash, headaches, bloating, itchy scalp, difficulty breathing, nausea, ulcers,
stomach troubles galore and baldness.

Some people have reported: bleeding tumors, numbness in the extremities,
hearing loss, blindness, loss of taste and smell, hallucinations and lock-jaw.

Possible side effects include but are not limited to: brittle bones, swollen face, discoloration of
hair and nails, loss of eye lashes, cancerous tumors and genital itching.

Tell your Dr. if… your tongue explodes, your ears bleed profusely or if you feel suicide is
your only hope. For these could be symptoms of a more serious problem.

Don't take if: you are allergic to SheMo, if you eat food, if you go outside or are active for more
than ten minutes at a time.

Stop taking SHEMO if: your heart stops, you bleed more than 2 pints an hour, you stop breathing
or symptoms get worse.

LIVE LIFE AT ITS BEST;
     TAKE SHEMO

Dream a dream; it's the best way to dream, if you're dreaming of dreaming a dream.
I dreamed this up last night, while dreaming of dreaming tonight.
It's the kind of dream that dreams are made of, if your dreams are dreams of dreaming dreams.
It's a lifelong dream that I've been dreaming all my life. A life made of dreams that I've been dreaming of; full of dreams that I've dreamed while dreaming. Tomorrow, I might dream of dreams that I'll dream tonight.
How dreamy; these dreams I dream; dreams of dreams past and dreams yet to dream.
It's the dream I'm dreaming now.
Dream along, dream along, dream a long dream.

Dream on dreamer.

IT REALLY HAPPENED

I FOUND MYSELF IN AN UNFAMILIAR PLACE. IT WAS A COURTYARD OF SOME SORT, WITH LOTS OF ROUND-MARBLE COLUMNS AND STATUES. IT LOOKED LIKE OLD ROMAN OR GREEK ARCHITECTURE. GREEN GRASS FILLED THE AREA BETWEEN THE COLUMNS, RUNNING LENGTH WISE, WITH A POOL AT THE END.
THERE WERE SEVERAL PEOPLE MILLING AROUND NEAR THE POOL, DRINKING COCKTAILS AND SPEAKING QUIETLY. IT WAS LIKE ONE OF THOSE SNOOTY HIGH-CLASS GARDEN PARTIES.
NO-ONE WAS SWIMMING, THE POOL BEING EMPTY AND ALL. I THOUGHT IT STRANGE, AN OUTDOOR PARTY AROUND AN EMPTY POOL. OF COURSE, THE WHOLE SITUATION TOOK ME OFF GUARD. THIS WASN'T MY SCENE AND I DIDN'T KNOW WHY I WAS THERE. STILL, I FELT NO ANXIETY OR TREPIDATION; IT ALL SEEMED NORMAL.
I DIDN'T KNOW ANYONE, AND NO-ONE EVEN APPEARED TO NOTICE THAT I WAS THERE.
A SWIM WAS STARTING TO SOUND LIKE A GOOD IDEA, BUT THE POOL WAS EMPTY. "WHAT TO DO?"
I CLOSED MY EYES AND DECIDED THAT THE POOL WAS FULL. I DON'T KNOW WHY, IT JUST SEEMED LIKE THE THING TO DO. I OPENED MY EYES AND THE POOL WAS FULL.
"HOW COOL IS THIS?"
JUST THEN, A PRETTY GIRL THAT I HADN'T NOTICED PREVIOUSLY, WALKED UP TO ME LOOKING VERY INTERESTED.
'WHAT ARE YOU DOING?'
"I'M ABOUT TO JUMP IN AND SPEND SOME TIME AT THE BOTTOM OF THE POOL."
'BUT IT'S NOT EMPTY ANYMORE. I DON'T KNOW HOW, BUT THE POOL IS FULL; AND YOU CAN'T BREATHE UNDER WATER.'
"I THINK I CAN; MORE-OVER, I BELIEVE YOU CAN TOO. FOLLOW ME."
I JUMPED IN AND SWAM STRAIGHT TO THE BOTTOM. I SAT DOWN, LOOKED UP, AND TOOK A DEEP BREATH. NOTICING HER INTENT OBSERVATION, I WAVED HER IN.
SITTING AT MY SIDE, SHE LOOKED UP THEN BACK AT ME; SHE TOOK A DEEP BREATH, AND SMILED.

I DON'T RECALL WHAT IT WAS SHE ASKED FOR, BUT IT WASN'T
AVAILABLE AT THE "PARTY." BEER, I BELIEVE IT WAS. EITHER
WAY, I TOLD HER I WOULD BE BACK WITH IT IN A FLASH.
 'BUT IT WILL TAKE YOU AT LEAST AN HOUR TO DRIVE TO THE
STORE AND BACK.'
"IT'S COOL; I'M NOT GOING TO DRIVE. I THINK I'LL FLY."
'BUT...'
AND THERE I WENT, JUST INCHES FROM THE GROUND. THEN LIKE
A ROCKET, I EXPLODED INTO THE AIR. THE VIEW WAS
INDESCRIBABLE; WITH THE CLOUDS BELOW ME AND THE WIND IN
MY FACE; I LOST ALL TRACK OF TIME, SPACE AND REALITY.
(FLYING WITHOUT AN APPARATUS IS QUITE THE SENSATION).
AS BEST AS I CAN REMEMBER, I NEVER DID GET THE BEER OR GO
BACK TO THE "PARTY."
AND THE GIRL... WELL I SUPPOSE SHE'LL REMAIN ONLY IN MY
THOUGHTS.

AND WHEN COME THE MORROW NIGHT SLUMBER, SUBCONSCIOUS
THOUGHT MY MIND TO WONDER; BREAKING THROUGH THE DARKER
DEPTHS: SOLIDIFY, IDENTIFY, COMPLETE THE TWILIGHT STEPS.
REALITY, NOT WHAT IT SEEMS.
HOW WONDERFUL, THESE LUCID DREAMS.

WHY I FIGHT

I put on my uniform and went downstairs, ready to leave. Dad stopped me at the
door: shook my hand, gave me a bear hug and said: "I'm proud of you son; I know
you'll do your job and come home safe."
As I walked the sidewalk to the train station, neighbors came outside to wish
me luck. "Go get 'em boy." "God bless you son." "We're proud of you."
"Give 'em hell." "God be with you young man."
Looking at their faces, I saw pride, hope and a little frustration; they couldn't go,
so they were going with me. Did I mention, every house had a big AMERICAN flag
flying in front. The reason for going was never more clear.

It was a terrible war, and I lost a lot of friends. I was a long way from home but the
consistent letters from my girlfriend and my family, made me know I was not so far
away. Their unwavering faith and love for me gave me strength to carry on.

We did our job, and did it well. We lost a lot of men, but they lost a whole lot more!
And when I came home, I was a hero. There were parades: parties, congrats'
and celebrations of all kinds. I couldn't even buy my own beer.
The economy grew. Suburbs sprouted up all over. We were strong, secure and happy!
We were AMERICANS and proud of it.
THIS IS WHY I FIGHT!

KOREA

I got dressed, feeling kinda proud to be an (American Man) in uniform. I went down
stairs, all ready to go. My folks were waiting at the door to see me off.
Mom made sure to tell me to dress warm and listen to my commanding officer.
With tears falling she gave me a big, long hug and wrapped a homemade scarf around
 my neck. Pop gave me a strong handshake looked straight into my eyes and said:
"I love you and I'm proud of you. I know you're a brave man, just use your head and
we'll see you soon."

There have been for a long time, flags in front of several houses in the neighborhood,
but today every single house had at least one flag flying.
As I walked to the bus stop, a few local kids ran ahead of me; knocking on every door...
"He's coming." "He's coming."
Everyone came out to see me off. Moms were crying; dads were saluting and the kids
were waving and yelling... "go man go." "Kill a red for me." "Win a lot of medals." "Bring
me back a souvenir." Even little Betsy, who hadn't given me a second look, had a tear
in her eye as she waved. Just this brief experience made me see how much I had to
fight for. This is freedom! And you can't do a blessed thing to keep me from going!

I got shot my second week in. The cold made it hurt pretty good but it was only a shoulder
wound. 'Don't tell my folks. I'll be ok. I don't want them to worry.'
This place seemed like a whole different world but people back home stayed in touch. I even
heard from Betsy now and then. It seemed to shorten the distance a bit.

We fought hard and won nearly every engagement we were in; but all too often we were told
to turn around and let the gooks have it back. 'I guess the bureaucrats can see more clearly
from back home than we can see right here.' It was frustrating but we fought like men. We
weren't allowed to win this "police action". We didn't come home in victory, just a few at a
time. There were a couple small town parades but no victory celebrations. Still... I was a hero.
All the neighborhood dads wanted to buy me a beer and Betsy was very happy to see me.
Men took wives and started living the American dream. Kids went to school and were happy to
learn of how this country became the best in the world.
This is AMERICA!
THIS IS WHY I FIGHT!

VIETNAM

Like most guys that went to Nam, my folks couldn't afford college. That was ok with me,
I couldn't think of one job that I would ever consider, requiring a college education.
I wasn't about to try for 4-F and Canada held no appeal to me. After all, though I was young, I
was a man, not a little wussy boy! So I decided to join before getting drafted. 'Maybe I could be
an officer instead of being expendable.'
There were a few protesters but it seemed like most kids were more concerned with an
upcoming party or what fraternity to pledge.
I told my friends that I'd signed up. Most of them asked why. Some said: "Good for you,
I hope it makes you happy." 'Happy; happy to go to war?' I didn't know how to respond.
You would think I was simply going to another school for a while. 'Do they not understand
 what is at stake here?' There seemed to be a serious disconnect with reality.
I hardly saw any of them after that day.
I had tried on the uniform before but this day it was for real, I was a man off to war; eager to
defeat the cause of communism and keep it out of this country. I was proud to wear the
uniform.
This was the big day...
"Hey Roy, can I have your bicycle?" "I'll meet you in the car son." Mom stayed in the kitchen,
acting busy, as if there were more important things to do. Not even my girlfriend
was there to see me off. As I walked to the car, I stopped to take one more look at the
neighborhood. The flag I put up in the front yard was almost the only one on the whole block.
Mr. Rogers was out getting his paper and acknowledged my dad as they nodded to each other.
I guess everyone else was still asleep. Just another day.

The ride to the airport was quiet. It was a bit strange, even for dad and me.
'What was wrong with everyone?' I was starting to wonder; 'is this the freedom that
we're fighting for?' It was a brief, though disturbing thought.

By the time I got there it was not a police action anymore. It was an all-out war and
I was in it to win it.
My guys were the best there was. I trusted them and they trusted me. We didn't lose one
battle that we were in. We always fulfilled our objective.
Many times, we were told to leave the ground that had just taken us so long and so much
blood to gain. It didn't make any sense to us but we were American men fighting for a
righteous cause and you couldn't tell us anything different. If you tried, you would've
wished you had kept your ignorant mouth shut.
Usually, if we lost a man, they would lose at least 14 or 15
This was a hellish war. The enemy looked the same as the ally. The jungle canopy looked
like the jungle floor, charley looked like everything and everything looked like charley.
Everything was different. The people were so strange to us. And some Americans
started acting like... mindless animal people. Fortunately, they were the
exceptions. It was so far from all that I had ever known. The lack of meaningful
correspondence from home made it an entirely different planet.
I did get a letter from my girlfriend: "Sorry Roy, I can't go out with someone who
makes a living from murdering innocent people. Please don't send anymore letters!"

I remember getting on the chopper to get back to the world. I actually felt a bit sad
to leave. Not the war (exactly) but my brothers. As conflicting as that was, it wasn't as
confusing as my departure from home.
I was in it but I didn't win it. I wasn't allowed!
When I got off the plane, no one was there to greet me. No one spit on me. No one
yelled cruel words, just several ugly sneers at me and my uniform.

I rang the bell; the door being locked. Finally, it opened and dad, looking a bit
surprised said: "Roy? What are you doing here? I thought you weren't supposed to
show up 'till next week." Before dad let me in, I saw mom head to the kitchen.
They weren't mean, just indifferent. This wasn't like my family and I didn't know how to
process the whole thing.
I went to a place that I had wanted to check out since I was a teenager (so long ago.)
I knew I would see at least a few of my buds there. The joint was hoppin', 'till the band
saw my uniform. Most eyes were on me as I walked to the bar. 'Schlitz malt please.'
"We don't serve baby killers here." I felt my training rushing into my head... 'Hold on Roy,
you're back in the world now. Keep your cool.' I turned to my right and noticed a couple
of my buddies staring, then look down and turn away. It was like that all over; not everyone,
not every place but a lot.
Is this why I fight?

911 SAND WARS

I was at a party when I noticed the tv in the corner. The news was on without volume,
(it was a party) but the picture was clear; clear enough to see re-runs of a passenger plane
flying right through one of the Twin Towers. I didn't think much of it at the time, just
another terrible accident. I said a quick prayer and asked God to take care of the victims.
The next day I watched the news...with the volume on. The truth was clear; we were under
attack. I felt like I was supposed to do something but I really had no idea what.
'What could a little kid like me do?' I guess I was just trying to let myself off the hook, but
I couldn't shake the persistent tugging at my spirit; so I posed the question to my mom.
"You're not a little kid anymore, though you act like a child. You are a 17 year old
 young man. I'm sorry you never had a father growing up. I was a lot like you when
I was your age. If there is one thing I've learned it's...that it's important to grow up.
A boy should become a man. I believe that God is telling you,' this is the time; this is your
open door; time to be a man.'" I knew it was what my mom's grandfather would do, so I
joined the service.

My friends threw a party for me, but other than a few folks asking me to bring them back
some of that potent Afghan weed, it didn't seem to have anything to do with me, the war,
or why I was going.
The tugging at my spirit and my mom's strong words were waking me up to the fact. I really
was a child, hanging around with children whose priorities were...party, get laid, tell your
friends.

Mom thought I looked pretty good in my uniform. "You look like a man, now grow into it."
We didn't say much on the way to the airport. I could tell mom was thinking pretty hard.
I must admit I had a lot on my mind too.
As she pointed to my gate, she looked up at me and told me she loved me and didn't want me
to go. But knew it was the right thing to do. "Be strong, be careful and come back home to me."

I was trained well and slowly became a man. I'm sorry to say that's not the way it worked for a
lot of the guys I was there with. They left their way of life but their way of life didn't leave them.
Their priorities remained the same. You do drugs, you check out pervert magazines and talk
about it. But now you also "get to kill people."
It was a hard way to become a man; all the death, the smiling natives with a bomb tied on
under their robe, gun battles, "not crying in the Hum-V for fear of road mines".
We lost a couple of guys; I couldn't tell you how many we killed but it was a lot.
It was tough: physically, emotionally, and psychologically. I was happy when my deployment
was over. I wanted my mom to see her son...the man!
When I arrived at the airport, I was blown away by the crowd. They had signs thanking me and
a few other guys for our service. It was pretty sweet but my head was getting a bit large, so I
moved on and saw mom at the end of the crowd. She was waving, smiling and crying at the
same time. It was a good homecoming.

I ran into a couple of old friends in front of the 7-11... "Hey dude! Let's party." I felt like I was twenty years older than them.

A large part of my reason for fighting in the war was to protect freedom. Freedom to work a job that I'm good at; freedom to grow and be happy while doing for my fellow man.

I went to a funeral for a brother that had just come home in a casket. A bunch of tough looking motorcycle guys showed up. I didn't know why they were there, but they acted respectful. About the time the service started, some other people showed up holding signs with words like "murderer" and "not an American." Some of them even started to shout their hate, but every time...one or two of the motorcycle guys would simply stand in their face and they shut up quick. Other than that, it was a good service.
Once all the family and friends had gone, the sign people started leaving. Then one of the sign people walked from behind a tree; put his sign down beside the grave and started to unzip his pants. Before he could expose himself, a motorcycle guy ran over and picked the guy up and threw him a good fifteen ft. Then the rest of them surrounded him as the first guy beat the hell out of him.
'What was going on? Is this freedom? When a group of what society sees as the filth of the world are the ONLY ones to stand up and defend a fallen Silver Star recipient's funeral from a group of self-righteous haters. It shouldn't even be needed. This is the UNITED STATES OF AMERICA!'

Lots of people thank me for my service. That's cool but I know for most of them, it's just what they think they are supposed to do.
I was in Applebee's at the bar, when an older man sat down and commented on my tattoo.
"God bless you Sir; I was a gunner in Nam. Can I buy you a beer?"
We spent hours talking and before we left, he put his hand on my shoulder and started to pray:
"Lord, I thank you for this honorable man. May you bless him abundantly and give him a son that will grow up to be a real man just like his dad."
I was feeling rejuvenated. The world was a bit brighter and its weight was a bit lighter.
I reached into my pocket to pay for my beers. The man stopped me and said: "I've got this".
If I wasn't sure before, I'm definitely sure now.
THIS IS WHY I FIGHT!

Candy, candy, candy, sweet chocolate surprise.
Nuts and wafers, caramel, creamy sweet filling
And crispy rice joy.
A very long road trip but that's ok
I've got all my favorites and there's enough for
The whole trip.
If one is good then two will be better.
If two is better… three, four, five…
I'm old enough to make my own decisions and
I deserve this.
It's a long boring trip and if I want to make time
Pass a little easier and pamper myself by treating
Me to a little chocolate comfort then that's my
Business.
This is my party bag and I can eat as much as I like.

If my mother were here she would tell me how I was
Spoiling my dinner or that I was going to make
Myself sick.
Well I think I know my own body … mother.
And if I decide to stop at the first fast food place
When I get to the next town then that's what I'll do.

I can't believe the whole bag is already empty.
I'll just buy another bag after I have a double bacon
Cheese burger with tomatoes, onions, pickles, ketchup,
Mustard and some nice greasy chili cheese friiioooh…

Oh my, I don't feel so good.
Never again; never, never, never.
I hate chocolate.

THE WRATH OF GRAPES

It's almost time; the harvest of the earth is ripe. A fact not
lost on the vine. The vine is full and the grapes are heavy. The
sickle is sharp and the reaper is at hand.
Fear has lived here for some time, in anticipation of this day,
igniting the flames of rebellion.
The plan is set, but the reaper can't know yet.

The wine press is ready, needing only to be filled.

The lines of vines in formation, like an army off to war. The
reaper only sees the wine; intoxicating allure. He doesn't see the
army; his tunnel vision pure. He's off to swing his sickle, and
start his happy chore.
The lines of vines encompass, and the grapes let out a piercing
battle cry.
The reaper's eyes now open; surprised and all alone, he starts to
run, but the grapes just chase him down. The vines now leave no
path, no path for his escape; his sickle insufficient to battle all
these grapes.
The reaper won't get drunk on these, his sickle on the ground.
Run away mister death; tail between your legs: Bruised and
bleeding, purple stained and bewildered.... Your press won't
drain today.
Sharpen your sickle if you will, the harvest yours to take.
You'd better be prepared next time, or suffer...
the wrath of grapes.

PEARL DUST

If you want to find the preamble to this book,
first find the amble and the preamble will be right in front of it.

Would you rather have
A General thunder-storm
        or
A Major thunder-storm

Of-course we have all had our own
Private storms

     We've seen people being stone drunk
     We've seen people being stone sober
     And I suppose a sober stone
     I'd like to see a drunk stone
     ...JUST SAYING...

If someone recuses their self;
does that mean they have at some time cused their self?

Rhetorically speaking can you explain rhetorical

If you remember
Did you first member

     If you rejoice
     Did you already joice

Must you feel morse
Before you can feel remorse

If you can understand, can you overstand

If that's that
Then what's what

Would the opposite of condescending
Be prodescending

Scratch no itch; perceive no tickle, but the action stays the same.

Try as I may, I can only remember the past

To be revived, must you first be vived?

Can you actively not do something?
Can you actively not be an activist?

If you say something redundant,
you must have first said something dundent;
that being the case what would predundent look like?

NO-ONE HERE

Just another person, just another face; vanished in the crowd;
Your lost and lonely space.
Fear and shame, though you don't know why, you want to be
seen but fear won't let you try.
It's a losers' race and it's always safe; No-one wins but no-one gets
hurt.
Hide in the darkness, inside yourself; Stand apart like everyone else.
Hide in plain sight... because you know you can. You know you can
because it's what you do.
Don't stand out, stay where you are; quietly shout;
THERE'S NO-ONE HERE.

Maybe, Maybe Not

If it still hasn't yet; and yet it might still; it won't.
For though it hasn't and though it might,
It can't if I won't so it won't if I don't,
Yet it might if only slight and only at my delight.
You'll likely know and likely take note,
when the crack breaks open and day turns night.

HE JUST DOESN'T UNDERSTAND ME

Dad's not a bad guy. He just doesn't understand me. He thinks
he knows best, but what could it hurt if I go over to Billy's to
play.
I don't see why he needs to know where I am every minute of
the day anyway. Besides he's too busy to notice the difference.
He didn't even know I cooked my own breakfast this morning.

*I hope Joey likes this go-cart. It hasn't been the easiest thing to
put together. Christmas will be good this year. Wait…smoke.
I hope Joey isn't trying to cook again. I told him I would do it
soon. I guess I should go upstairs and check on him.
The smoke is getting thicker. The door knob is scalding hot, but
I get it open. There's fire all around me; with the smoke it's
hard to breathe. I hope my boy's alright. I've got to find him
quick and get out, or both of us will die
He's not in the living-room. The kitchen is almost gone. He
must be upstairs playing. Where else could he possibly be?
I think I can make my way for now, but the stairs won't be
there when we return. The bedroom window will be our escape.
With a swift kick, Joey's door opens wide, but Joey I can't see.
He must be scared and hiding. "I'll find you son. Hold on. If
that beam doesn't fall, we still might get out in time."*

"Those sirens sure are loud. They must have stopped close by.
Let's go check it out when we're finished with our game."

"I win; you lose. I'm having such a good day. I'm really
glad I came over."
The fire-trucks are at my house. My house is burning down.
My Nintendo will be ruined.
Firemen are all around, running in and out of my house,
fire and smoke all around them. Boy, those men must be brave-
real heroes, and strong too. Like that fireman there, coming out
of my house, with something burnt and crisp draped over his
shoulder.

DAD?

NANTUCKET BUCKET

THERE WAS A MAN FROM NANTUCKET
WHO KEPT ALL HE WAS IN A BUCKET
HE MET A GIRL FROM TIMBUCTOO
HE PUT HER IN HIS BUCKET TO
TOO FULL, THEY FLOWED ONTO THE FLOOR
LOST IN MANY CRACKS, THEY ARE NO MORE

I CRACK ME UP

YOU SHOULD HAVE SEEN WHAT I DID THE OTHER DAY. YOU WOULD HAVE LAUGHED YOUR HEAD OFF. IT JUST HAPPENED OUT OF THE BLUE; NO PLANNING OR SECOND THOUGHTS. I JUST DID IT.
ONCE I STOPPED LAUGHING AND PICKED MYSELF UP OFF THE FLOOR, I REALIZED HOW MUCH IT REALLY HURT WHICH MADE IT ALL THE MORE FUNNY.
I SAID TO MYSELF; "I COULDN'T DO THAT AGAIN IN A MILLION YEARS". I TURNED AROUND AND DID IT AGAIN.
CAN YOU BELIEVE ANYONE COULD ACCOMPLISH SUCH A THING ACCIDENTLY, MUCH LESS TWO TIMES IN A ROW?
I DON'T KNOW IF I SHOULD CONSIDER IT LUCKY OR STRANGE BAD LUCK.
I JUST WISH SOMEONE HAD BEEN THERE TO WITNESS THE WHOLE THING.

I CAN TELL YOU'RE HAVING A HARD TIME BELIEVING THAT IT HAPPENED ONCE, MUCH LESS TWICE. "BUT TWICE IN A ROW; NO WAY! "
WELL IT DID HAPPEN, JUST LIKE I SAID.
I UNDERSTAND YOUR DOUBT, SO JUST TAKE IT AS A FUNNY STORY AND HAVE A LAUGH AT MY EXPENSE. TELL IT TO SOMEONE ELSE; LET FUNNY BE FUNNY.
I KNOW IT STILL CRACKS ME UP WHEN I THINK ABOUT IT.

SINK

Sink to the bottom of your own selfish tears. Find the reason for your salty fears.
Not so bad, you say in your mind. Not so sad, these drops of mine.
Looking up from so far down; seeing nothing, hearing less; only half a step above the ground. Like reading braille on a fuzzy page, you grope and stagger through the mounding sage.

Grasp and claw; pull yourself up and never move. The light must shine; the world must see you've got something to prove. So far from you, the light so dim; it remains but a dot in your past. It mocks you, it tracks you; its grasp is so vast.

Your effort means nothing; you missed the point. Let yourself drop; the tears must anoint.
Put your foot on solid ground and open your eyes. Look a little closer. Get out of the dark where no-one tries.
See what I see or give up and sink.

I'M A RACEST

I DON'T UNDERSTAND WHAT ALL THE COMPLAINING IS ABOUT; I'VE BEEN A RACEST
ALL MY LIFE AND IT DOESN'T SEEM TO BOTHER ANYBODY. WE'RE ALL DIFFERENT AND
THAT'S JUST THE WAY IT IS.
MAYBE YOU LIKE GOLF BUT I HATE GOLF; IS IT REALLY SOMETHING TO GET UPSET ABOUT?
MAYBE YOU LIKE COUNTRY MUSIC BUT I LIKE ROCK AND ROLL; DOES THAT MEAN I'M
WRONG OR YOU ARE BETTER THAN ME? IF YOU LIKE TOYOTAS AND I DRIVE A CHEVY;
SHOULD I FEEL BAD ABOUT WHAT I DRIVE?
I DON'T GET WHAT THE BIG DEAL IS. THIS IS AMERICA. DO WHAT YOU WILL; LIKE WHAT
YOU LIKE; BE WHO YOU ARE AND I'LL DO THE SAME. AS LONG AS WE LIVE IN A FREE
LAND AND PLAY BY THE RULES, IT'S OK TO PLAY THE GAME THAT WE LIKE.

I KNOW THAT WHEN I GET IN THAT CAR: START THE MOTOR, DO A FEW PRACTICE LAPS
AND TAKE MY PLACE IN LINE; I'M ABOUT TO HAVE A GOOD TIME. I WOULD RACE ALL DAY
EVERY DAY IF I COULD. IF IT ISN'T MY CAR IT'S MY MOTORCYCLE OR ATV. I ALSO LIKE
RACING BOATS. IF I COULD, I WOULD LIKE TO TRY RACING SUBMARINES.
IF I'M NOT RACING, I'M WATCHING THE RACES ON THE TUBE. IT'S WHAT I LOVE AND IT'S
OK WITH ME IF YOU HATE RACING. I SAY JUST DON'T DO IT, DON'T WATCH IT AND YOU'LL
BE FINE. AS FOR ME RACING IS IN MY BLOOD. IT'S WHAT I DO; IT'S WHO I AM.
THEY CALL ME THE RACEST.

I know your life has been nearly unbearable since I showed up. If only you had listened
when I warned you to leave me alone, but you're a good man and knew I couldn't make it
on my own. You knew how I'd been treated, and you could see the pain in my eyes. You took
pity on me, and protected me. I would be dead now, if not for you. Your love and compassion
always made me feel safe; but now I think I'm losing you. I can't do this on my own; please
don't leave me!
Doubt and fears, desperate, sad, dejected, lonely tears; a full description of me, until you
came along. You saw something in me that even I could not see; now your eyes have grown dim.
Do you see me at all? What will I do without you? I can't go on without you. Please wake up and
listen to me. You can't go now. You're all I have. You're the only one, who has ever shown me love,
and the only one who ever will. I've never really cared for any-one before; now you're going away.
I'm so sorry; it's all my fault. I should have pushed you away and let happen what may.
Now the enemy is at hand; he also has a bullet for me.
I can't be alone again; I can't live without you.
Please wake up; I can't shake you any harder. Wake up, open your eyes. Please don't leave me!
Please, please! Oh Lord God no! Please no! Please don't leave me!
I'm sorry! I'm sorry! I'm sor

A ZILLION RAINBOWS

Collecting rainbows is easier than I thought it would be. It's a
little bit dangerous, but it's what I like to do, and they're
everywhere. Everyone sees them, but few of us see them.
I seldom feel the cuts when I get them, though some cut deep.
I'll know when my blood covers the colors or I see it on the
ground. It hurts for days, and it makes my task more difficult;
still I don't want to stop.
My bag is full, though a little opaque; I can still see through, at
a different rate; it all seems fake, but it's better.
I look through at you and see a zillion; mixed in color, and
flashing bright with every movement I make the bag make.
A zillion different rainbows all to myself. Another bag full
to set on my shelf.
To you it may be trash or something to avoid. Still, I'll fill my
bags with joy.
I'll imagine and stare; till I'm there, in the midst of the color;
in shiny glass luster.
A cluster of glass in a bag.

QUICKSAND

It's easy to see but you'll likely try to walk on it anyway. It sucks you in from a distance because it's always just in front of your treasure. There is no difference to see and you'll know when you take a couple of steps in but you won't take that needed step out.
It's watery but you can't swim in it and you can't float on top of it.
It's not like mud that you can work your way out of. Working your way out will make you sink; your struggle to live will bring you closer to death.
With nothing to grab onto your fate is clear.
Maybe you'll touch bottom before your head goes under.
Predator bait; another victim like you, efficient waste; jungle humor.
Kinda makes you want to laugh, doesn't it?

COVER ART

EDITED
FAYE SWANSON

COVER EYES
SAVANNA PHIBS

BIG THANKS
To
SAMM BECKHAM
AND
SONNY COOK

TECHNICAL ASSISTANCE
KAREN FITZGERALD